2.6

A Note to Parents and Caregivers:

With a focus on math, science, and social studies, *Read-it!* Readers support both the learning of content information and the extension of more complex reading skills. They encourage the development of problem-solving skills that help children expand their thinking.

 The PURPLE LEVEL presents basic topics and objects using high frequency words and simple language patterns.

 The RED LEVEL presents familiar topics using common words and repeating sentence patterns.

 The BLUE LEVEL presents new ideas using a larger vocabulary and varied sentence structure.

 The YELLOW LEVEL presents more challenging ideas, a broad vocabulary, and wide variety in sentence structure.

 The GREEN LEVEL presents more complex ideas, an extended vocabulary range, and expanded language structures.

 The ORANGE LEVEL presents a wide range of ideas and concepts using challenging vocabulary and complex language structures.

When sharing a content focused book with your child, read to find out facts and concepts, pausing often to restate and talk about the new information. The realistic story format provides an opportunity to talk about the language used, and to learn about reading to problem-solve for information. Encourage children to measure, make maps, and consider other situations that allow them to apply what they are learning.

There is no right or wrong way to share books with children. Find time to read and share new learning with your child, and pass on the legacy of literacy.

Adria F. Klein, Ph.D.
Professor Emeritus
California State University
San Bernardino, California

Editor: Shelly Lyons
Designer: Tracy Davies
Page Production: Michelle Biedscheid
Art Director: Nathan Gassman
Associate Managing Editor: Christianne Jones
The illustrations in this book were created with watercolor and colored pencil.

Picture Window Books
5115 Excelsior Boulevard
Suite 232
Minneapolis, MN 55416
877-845-8392
www.picturewindowbooks.com

Printed in the United States of America.

Library of Congress Cataloging-in-Publication Data
Gunderson, Jessica.
A stormy surprise / by Jessica Gunderson ; illustrated by Mernie Gallagher-Cole.
   p. cm. — (Read-it! readers: science)
ISBN-13: 978-1-4048-4223-6 (library binding)
[1. Electricity—Fiction.] I. Gallagher-Cole, Mernie, ill. II. Title.
PZ7.G963Sto 2008
[E]—dc22   2007032911

A STORMY Surprise

by Jessica Gunderson
illustrated by Mernie Gallagher-Cole

Special thanks to our advisers for their expertise:

Paul R. Ohmann, Ph.D.
Associate Professor of Physics
University of St. Thomas, St. Paul, Minnesota

Adria F. Klein, Ph.D.
Professor Emeritus, California State University
San Bernardino, California

PICTURE WINDOW BOOKS
Minneapolis, Minnesota

"Goodbye, Mom!" Ashley and Eric yelled as they waved to their mother.

"Well, kids," Dad said. "What do you want to do while Mom is gone?"

"Play football,"
Eric answered.

"Go swimming,"
Ashley said.

Dad looked up. Dark clouds rolled across the sky. "We'd better play indoors today," he said.

5

"Do we have to?" Eric asked.

"Staying inside is boring," Ashley moaned.

"It's not always boring," Dad said. "There's a surprise for you somewhere in the house. It's hidden in a dark place."

"The closet!" Ashley thought.

"The attic!" Eric thought.

Ashley and Eric ran into the house to find the big surprise.

Just as they were closing the front door, they saw a bolt of lightning zip through the sky. Thunder followed.

Another bolt of lightning flashed in the sky. Then the radio went quiet. The house became dark. The electricity had gone out.

Electricity is made up of small, charged particles that move in a path.

"Don't worry," Dad said. "That bolt of lightning must have hit a power line. Power lines send electricity from power stations to people's houses."

Power stations make electricity. The electricity moves through power lines to your house.

"How can we look for the surprise without any electricity in our house?" Ashley asked.

"We can use this!" Dad said. He grabbed a flashlight from a drawer in the kitchen.

12

"Good thing I bought new batteries," he said. "Now, let's find the surprise!"

To power a lightbulb with a battery, there must be a complete wire loop, or circuit. The circuit must run from the battery to the bulb and then back to the battery. Charged particles move through the circuit to the bulb. The bulb has a wire that heats up and glows when charged particles move through it.

Dad gave a flashlight to each of the children.
"We need another hint," Eric said. "The first
hint doesn't help. Every room is dark now."

"The surprise is in a place that starts with the
letter *B*," said Dad.

14

"I know where the surprise is!" Ashley yelled.
She pointed her flashlight down the hallway. She
began walking toward her bedroom. Eric and
Dad followed her.

When they got to Ashley's room, Dad asked, "Well, Ashley, where is the surprise?"

"Under a bed," Ashley replied.

They looked under Ashley's bed. They found lots of dolls, but no surprise.

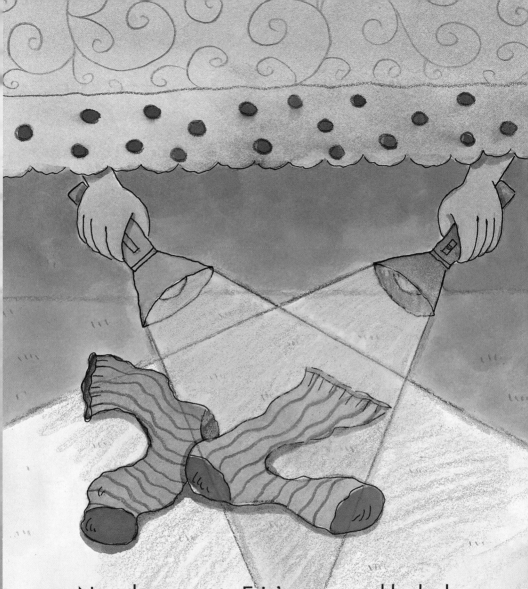

Next they went to Eric's room and looked under his bed. They found dirty socks, but no surprise. Then they went to Mom and Dad's room and looked under their bed. There was still no surprise.

"I'm tired of looking for the surprise," Eric groaned. "And I'm hungry."

18

"Can we bake a pizza?" Ashley asked.
"Not until the power comes on," Dad
answered. "The oven needs electricity to work."

Anything that plugs in or needs a
battery to work uses electricity.

"Nothing works without electricity," Eric said with a sigh.

"Your surprise doesn't need a battery or a power cord," Dad told him.

Wires carry electricity from the outlet to the object. Two wires are needed. One wire carries the electricity to the object. The other wire carries the electricity back to the outlet.

"So, it's not a remote-controlled car?" Eric asked.

"Nope," answered Dad.

"Or a radio?" asked Ashley.

"Nope," Dad said. "Let's keep searching. Where else should we look?"

The children shrugged. They were all out of ideas.

"Can you think of another room that begins with a *B*?" asked Dad.

Ashley and Eric looked at each other. "The basement!" they shouted.

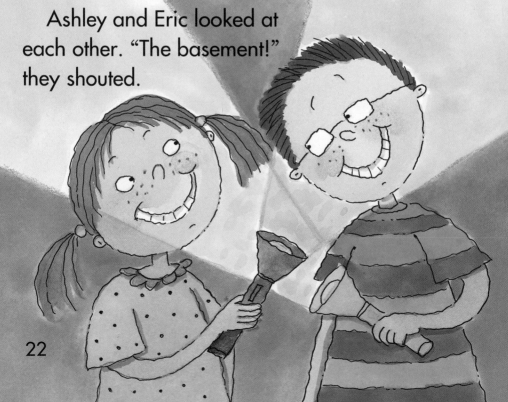

"Come on," Ashley said as she started walking toward the stairway.

Eric and Dad followed Ashley down the creaky stairs.

23

At the bottom of the stairs, Ashley pointed her flashlight at every corner. The basement was empty, except for a basket of dirty clothes and a large box.

"I don't see a surprise down here!" she announced.

Dad grinned and said, "You should look harder."

"Wait!" Eric said. "I hear something."

Ashley listened. All she could hear was the wind from the storm.

"It sounds like crying," Eric whispered.

"I don't hear it," Ashley said.

Eric pointed his flashlight in the direction of the noise.

"Look!" Ashley said. "That box is shaking!"
The children ran to the box. What could
be inside?

Ashley and Eric opened the box. "A kitten!" they cried.

Ashley lifted the kitten and cuddled it close.
Then the kitten leaped from Ashley's arms and
ran across the room.

"Wow, she's as fast as lightning!" Eric said.
"That's what her name will be," Ashley said.
"Lightning!"

Just then, the children heard another noise. It was the hum of electricity returning to the house. The radio played a song. Lights turned on upstairs.

As Ashley and Eric watched their new kitten play, they were glad the storm had kept them indoors. It hadn't been boring after all.

Electricity Activity

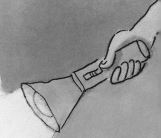

What you need:

- a balloon
- a wool sweater or blanket
- a sink with a faucet

What you do:

1. Blow up the balloon.
2. Rub the balloon on the wool sweater or blanket.
3. Hold the balloon next to your hair. What happens?
4. Rub the balloon on the wool.
5. Hold the balloon next to a wall. Let go. What happens?
6. Turn on the faucet so the water is running steadily but slowly.
7. Rub the balloon on the wool.
8. Hold the balloon next to the running water. What happens to the water?

Rubbing the balloon on the sweater creates static electricity. Static electricity makes your hair stand up and causes the balloon to stick to the wall. It even makes water move!

Glossary

circuit—the complete path that an electrical current can flow around
current—the flow of electricity
electricity—charged particles that move around a path
energy—the ability to do work or make things happen
particles—tiny pieces of matter in all things

To Learn More

More Books to Read

Hunter, Rebecca. *The Facts About Electricity*. North Mankato, Minn.: Smart Apple Media, 2005.

Olien, Rebecca. *Electricity*. Mankato, Minn.: Bridgestone Books, 2003.

Seuling, Barbara. *Flick a Switch: How Electricity Gets to Your Home*. New York: Holiday House, 2003.

Trumbauer, Lisa. *What Is Electricity?* New York: Children's Press, 2003.

On the Web

FactHound offers a safe, fun way to find Web sites related to topics in this book. All of the sites on FactHound have been researched by our staff.

1. Visit *www.facthound.com*
2. Type in this special code: 1404842233
3. Click on the FETCH IT button.

Your trusty FactHound will fetch the best sites for you!

Look for all of the books in the *Read-it!* Readers: Science series:

Friends and Flowers (life science: bulbs)
The Grass Patch Project (life science: grass)
The Sunflower Farmer (life science: sunflowers)
Surprising Beans (life science: beans)

The Moving Carnival (physical science: motion)
A Secret Matter (physical science: matter)
A Stormy Surprise (physical science: electricity)
Up, Up in the Air (physical science: air)